What's Next, Nina?

by Sue Kassirer
Illustrated by Page Eastburn O'Rourke

The Kane Press
New York

Book Design/Art Direction: Roberta Pressel

Library of Congress Cataloging-in-Publication Data

Kassirer, Sue.
    What's next, Nina? / by Sue Kassirer ; illustrated by Page O'Rourke.
    p. cm. — (Math matters.)
    Summary: When the string of a borrowed necklace breaks, Nina must quickly get the beads back in order and restrung before her sister finds out.
    ISBN 1-57565-106-8 (alk. paper)
    [1. Sequences (Mathematics)—Fiction. 2. Pattern perception—Fiction. 3. Parties—Fiction. 4. Sisters—Fiction.] I. O'Rourke, Page Eastburn, ill. II. Title. III. Series.
    PZ7.K1562 Wf 2001
    [E]—dc21   01-029393
                                                                    CIP
                                                                    AC

10 9 8 7 6 5 4 3 2 1

First published in the United States of America in 2001 by The Kane Press.
Printed in Hong Kong.

MATH MATTERS is a registered trademark of The Kane Press.

It's today—the big fancy party. And all I've got to wear is a plain old dress. What am I going to do?

3

I guess it's my own fault. I went shopping for a new dress, but then I saw a cool skateboard. And I really wanted it.

"Sorry, Nina," Mom said, "you can get a skateboard *or* a new dress—not both."

So I said, "Okay, I'll just wear one of my old dresses to the party." That didn't seem so bad. Until today.

It turns out the only dress that still fits is this icky plain one. How can I go like this? Everybody else will be wearing their fanciest party clothes!

Then I see a necklace on my sister Julia's dresser. It's beautiful. There are sky blue and misty purple beads, and pearly pink and orange ones. Sunset colors.

Quickly, I try the necklace on—and right away, I look fancy. I've just got to wear it.

I should ask Julia if I can borrow it—but she'll probably say no. Anyway, I shouldn't bother her right now. She's busy playing CDs with her friends. Hey! I'll bet I can borrow the necklace and put it back before she even misses it!

I tiptoe into the hall.
Good! The coast is clear!
I make a mad dash down
the stairs.

I throw on my coat
and scarf. "Ready, Mom!"
I call out.

9

Sure enough, all the girls at the party look fancy. But no one notices that my dress is plain. They're all too busy admiring my necklace. Everyone is crazy about it.

Only Alice knows that it's my sister's. Alice is my best friend. We tell each other everything.

We have a great time at the party. There's a magician who pulls rabbits out of a hat, a special ice-cream punch, and a cake that looks like a castle!

Alice and I are ready to leave when I
feel a tickle on my neck. I reach up. No!
It can't be! The necklace is breaking!
Beads are flying all over the place.

Everyone runs after them. I just stand
there holding onto what's left of the
necklace—three little beads. All I can
think is, "What will I tell Julia? Why did
I ever take it?"

"I think we've got them all!" says
Alice. "Let's ask my mom to drop us at
that new bead store. Maybe someone
there can help you put it back together."

"Do you think they could?" I ask.

"Sure!" says Alice. "Beads are their business!"

Then there's hope! I thank everyone for helping, and off we go.

What a store! The walls are covered with beautiful necklaces, earrings, and bracelets. There are lots of cubbies filled with beads. And the beads are every size, color, and shape in the universe!

Now, if I can just remember how the
necklace looked....

"Can I help you girls?" asks Betsy, the owner.

I spill out my story—and my beads. "They're all mixed up," I tell her, "except for these three."

"Those three beads are a clue," Betsy says. "Look at this." She holds out a bracelet. "Blue, blue, red, gold. Blue, blue, red, gold…"

"It's a pattern!" I say. "I guess my necklace had one too, right?"

"Exactly!" says Betsy.

Betsy sweeps my beads into a basket and hands me a funny-looking tray. "You can use this to work out your pattern," she says.

I take a deep breath. "Pattern…pattern…" I say. "How did it go?"

"Another purple?" asks Alice.

"No…, there was more blue," I say.

"Lots more!" says Alice.

I try a blue bead.

I put down another
and another.

"Looking good!" Alice says.

Whoops! Where did that purple
bead go?

Alice and I do purple, purple, blue, blue, blue, blue again and again. *Whew!* "I know what I'll dream about tonight," I say.

"Me, too!" says Alice.

At last all the blue and purple beads are used up. "What's next?" Alice asks.

"The pink and orange beads," I say. "But I
don't remember the pattern."

"I don't either," says Alice. "And my mom
will be here soon. It's getting late."

I look out the window. Sure enough, the
sun is going down.

"That's it!" I shout. "The necklace made
me think of a sunset!"

"Yes!" says Alice. "There was even a gold bead—like the sun."

"But it's not here," I moan. "It must be lost." I slump in my chair.

"No problem," Alice says. "We're in a bead store, remember?"

Alice brings me a whole bunch of gold beads. One is just perfect! I put it in the tray. "And now," I say.

"Pink and then orange," Alice says, "like in the sunset."

I put down all the pink beads and all the orange beads.

Yay! We did it!

Alice helps me string the beads. Then she fastens the necklace.

"It's as good as new!" I say.

Back home, I tiptoe upstairs and put the necklace on Julia's dresser. You'd think I'd feel okay now, right? But I don't. I never should have taken it—not without asking.

"How was the party?" asks Julia.

"Oh, Julia," I say. I take a big breath. "I'm so sorry I took your necklace and wore it to Tiffany's party, and I didn't ask you, and it was just so beautiful, and my dress was so plain—"

"It sure was!" says Julia. "That's why I got you the necklace. But you ran out of here so fast, I couldn't tell you."

"What?" I say. "It was for me?" I can hardly speak.

"I got one for myself, too," Julia says. "It's just the same, see?"

I stare hard at my sister's necklace.
"Well, it's almost the same...," I say.
"But yours has five blues and one
purple. And on the bottom..."

"Wow, you have an eye for patterns!" says Julia. "You could make your own jewelry. Did you know there's a brand new bead shop in town?"

I start to laugh. And then I tell Julia just how I got so good at patterns!

PATTERNS CHART

I can draw patterns with color, size, and shape! Try it! It's fun!

Color Pattern

Pattern: green, green, green, yellow, yellow, red

Size Pattern

Pattern: small, large, small, small, large, large

Color <u>and</u> Size Pattern

Pattern: small yellow, small yellow, large yellow, small purple, small purple, large purple

Color <u>and</u> Shape Pattern

Pattern: red circle, yellow square, blue circle, green square